BASKETBALL
SPARKPLUG

Books by Matt Christopher

BASKETBALL SPARKPLUG

by
Matt
Christopher

Illustrated by
Ken Wagner

Little, Brown and Company *Boston Toronto*

LIBRARY OF CONGRESS CATALOG CARD NO. 57-8038

00208 07 01

Eleventh Printing

*Published simultaneously in Canada
by Little, Brown & Company (Canada) Limited*

PRINTED IN THE UNITED STATES OF AMERICA

BASKETBALL
SPARKPLUG

To Duane

1

KIM looked at the scoreboard.

ARROWS — 41, COMETS — 43.

He turned back to the game and leaned his elbows on his bare knees. He had played the first quarter and had scored six points. That wasn't bad. But he could not understand Coach Joe Stickles.

The coach had started Bobbie Leonard in Kim's place in the second quarter. The third quarter had just begun, and Bobbie was still in the game. However, the coach must know what he was doing.

Allan Vargo, the Arrows' center and tallest player, dribbled the ball down-court. Just before the foul line and to the right of it, he came to a quick stop. The Comet player who guarded him flashed by. Allan lifted the basketball above his head, his fingers and thumbs spread far apart. With a spring of his long, thin body the ball left his hands and sailed in an arch for the basket.

The ball dropped in without touching the rim! For a second it fluttered against the net, then fell through.

The crowd's yell filled the school gym. Allan's shot had tied the score!

Kim felt a tingle of excitement. So far the Arrows had lost two games and won one. If they took this game they would have two wins and two losses, and they would be in third place in the Small Fry Basketball League.

But Kim didn't really care too much about that. He didn't even care too much whether they ended in first place, or last. What he wanted more than anything was just to play basketball.

"Kim!"

He met Coach Joe Stickles's sharp gray eyes. The coach was a small, chunky man with very little hair on his head.

"Report to the bench, Kim, and take Bobbie's place!"

"Okay!"

Kim reported to the scorekeeper. A few seconds later the referee blew his whistle and Kim ran onto the court.

He tapped Bobbie on the shoulder. "Your turn to warm the bench, Bobbie!" He smiled.

"Okay!" said Bobbie. He was a small, husky-legged boy with a crew cut. He pointed to the man Kim was to cover, and ran off the court.

The whistle blew again for time in. The referee tossed the ball to a Comet player standing outside the white line. Since he was Ron Tikula's man, Ron covered him.

Kim tried to watch the boy with the ball and the boy he guarded at the same time. His man was on the go every second, darting every which way like a rabbit. Kim tried to keep between the two players so that if the ball was thrown to his man he could catch it.

All at once his man leaped in front of him and caught the ball! Kim scampered after him. His sneakers slipped and he almost fell. He caught himself and went after the Comet player, who was running upcourt. Kim's solid white legs looked like bright winking lights. His thick blond hair bobbed on his head as if it would shake off.

He couldn't let that man make a basket. He just couldn't. The Comets would shoot ahead and Coach Joe Stickles would blame him.

Kim caught up with the Comet player. He tried to get his right hand around

the boy's waist to hit the ball. A loud *smack!* sounded. He had slapped the boy's wrist instead of the ball.

"*Shr-i-e-k!*"

The referee's whistle pierced the hall. A finger went up high.

Kim stared. A foul!

2

SOMEONE squeezed his arm. "Come on, O'Connor!" an angry voice snapped. "Watch what you're doing! This ain't no choir!"

Kim caught Ron Tikula's disgusted look. Ron was taller and heavier than Kim. His hair was coal black, like his eyes.

Kim's face reddened. He looked away.

"Get down there, Kim!" a voice shouted. "Get down there!"

The voice jerked him out of his thoughts. He glanced toward the bench.

Coach Stickles was making motions for him to move upcourt. He sprang into a run. He got into position under the backboard, and kept his toes just outside the white line. The referee held up his hand. It came down like a signal arm at a railroad crossing. At the same time his whistle shrilled.

The Comet player shot. The ball sailed directly through the hoop, hitting the net like a whisper.

Jimmie Burdette, who stood across from Kim, ran behind him and gave him a friendly tap on the hip. "Don't let that bother you, Kim! We'll get 'em!"

"Yeah," Kim murmured. He knew that Jimmie was just trying to perk him up.

Dutchie McBride dribbled the ball halfway down-court, then passed to Allan. Allan shot to Jimmie, who faked a pass, then leaped for a hook shot. The crowd screamed as the ball banked against the backboard, touched the rim, and rolled over.

"Tough luck, Jimmie!" cried Kim.

He rushed in to get the ball. He fell on it. At the same time a Comet player tried to pull it from him. The whistle shrilled for a jump ball.

The referee tossed the ball into the air. The Comet player outjumped Kim and tapped the ball. Allan Vargo snared it from a Comet's hands. He pivoted, then shot a short pass to Ron.

Kim was in the open. "Here!" he shouted.

He didn't think Ron would throw the ball to him. Ron and Dutchie were two boys who teased him about singing in the church choir. But Ron did throw the ball, and Kim caught it.

Kim stood, puzzled, inside the white circle in the middle of the court. No one was near him. Somebody in the stands shouted, "Shoot! Shoot!"

Kim looked at Jimmie, Allan, and the others. They were well guarded. He looked at the basket.

It was a long way to throw. But at any second the quarter might end.

The Arrows were one point behind.

He was responsible for that point. If he shot and made it the Arrows would go into the lead. A lot of guys made shots from the middle of the court.

Kim brought the big, round ball up against his chest, both his hands spread wide behind it. One of the Comets saw he was going to shoot, and sped toward him. Kim leaped. The ball shot from his hands. It just missed the tips of the Comet player's fingers.

The ball sailed through the air close to the white ceiling, then curved down toward the basket. There was a hush in the gym. Then a terrific roar as the ball sailed *over* the backboard!

Ron's voice screamed at him. "Pass

14

that ball! Who do you think you are? Wally Goodrich?"

Wally Goodrich was a professional basketball player with the Seacord Lions. Kim always talked about him.

Time was called. A familiar horn sounded from the bench. Bobbie Leonard was coming back in to replace Kim.

Kim ran off the court. He kept his eyes down. He hardly noticed the sweat that rolled into them.

"That's pretty far to shoot, Kim," Coach Stickles said. "Try to pass when you can." Then he leaned over and patted Kim on the knee. "Don't let it bother you, kid. Cheer up."

Then the quarter ended.

3

THE two minutes went by quickly. The sweat on Kim's body had hardly dried.

A Comet player threw in the ball from outside the out-of-bounds line. His teammate caught it and heaved a long pass upcourt.

"Get up there! Get up there!" Coach Stickles shouted. Kim wondered if anybody could miss hearing that strong, powerful voice.

A Comet player, alone under the basket, caught the pass and made a perfect layup shot. Kim saw that the player was Bobbie's man.

The scoreboard flashed the score: ARROWS — 43, COMETS — 46.

The game was close. But the Arrows still had a chance. Kim wished he could get in again. He would never have let his man be alone as Bobbie had.

A Comet player caught a pass Allan had meant for Ron Tikula, and dribbled down to the circle in the middle of the court. Jimmie Burdette made a few stabs at the ball, then hurried upcourt to cover his man.

Kim grinned. Jimmie Burdette was a good player. Not only that, he was a nice kid too. You never heard him argue. You never saw him play dirty.

17

Kim was glad that Jimmie Burdette and he were good pals.

The Comet player was standing in the white circle — the same spot in which Kim had stood a few minutes before.

The Comet player glanced at the basket. He was tall, about five feet six or seven. He set himself for the long shot. His knees bent, then straightened. The ball flipped from his hands. It was a perfect throw. It hit the backboard and bounded through the hoop for two points.

Everybody — even the Arrows' rooters — gave him a hand.

The Arrows showed some fight after that. Kim got in and scored a set shot. Then Ron made a neat break, followed by a quick drive in which netted them two more points.

On the next play Ron fouled. Coach Stickles took him out because it was Ron's fourth foul. One more and he would be out for good.

The Comets made the free throw, putting them ahead 49 to 47.

Dutchie passed the ball from out of bounds to Kim. A Comet player swept in like a bolt of lightning, caught the ball, and dribbled upcourt. He stopped suddenly and hurled the ball to a teammate waiting under the basket. The player caught it and dumped it in easily.

Kim took out the ball, tossed it to Dutchie. The Comet guard rushed in and tried to pull the ball from Dutchie's hands. They pulled and tugged, but neither let go of the ball.

The whistle shrilled.

"Jump!" cried the referee, the whistle bouncing against his chest as he ran forward.

The thin, long-legged Comet player outjumped Dutchie easily. He tapped the ball to a redheaded teammate who dribbled part way up the court, then passed the ball. Another Comet snared it, stopped quickly, and tried a set shot. The ball sailed through the air and into the basket.

Kim groaned.

"Go in, Ron!" said Coach Stickles.

Ron went in. Jimmie Burdette passed the ball to him. Ron dribbled to the

center of the court and bounced the ball to Dutchie, who threw it to Kim. Kim snapped it to Jimmie, who was running toward the basket. A Comet player intercepted it, dribbled upcourt, then passed.

The ball hit Dutchie's outstretched hand and started bouncing toward the out-of-bounds line when the horn blew, ending the game.

The Arrows lost, 53 to 47.

4

AFTER supper Ron Tikula and Jimmie Burdette came over to Kim's house. Kim could hear them talking as they approached on the cement walk.

"Hi," he said, as he opened the door.

"Hi, Kim," Jimmie said. He and Ron wore dungarees and jackets. Both were carrying sneakers. Ron was bareheaded, but Jimmie was wearing a blue baseball cap with the letter B on it. B stood for Brooklyn, Jimmie's favorite baseball team.

"Can you come down to the gym?" Jimmie asked. "Or are you still tired?"

Kim smiled. "No, I'm not tired. Going to practice?"

"Naturally," spoke up Ron. A crooked grin spread on his lips.

Kim looked at him, then looked back at Jimmie. "Wait a minute. I'll ask my mother."

He left the door part way open and started for the dining room. He stopped as his mother came into the kitchen. She was wearing a white lace apron over a blue house dress.

"What is it, Kim?" she asked. Her blue eyes were exactly the color of his.

"Jimmie and Ron are here. They want me to go down to the gym with them."

She came closer and ran her fingers through his thatch of blond hair.

"Did you tell them you couldn't go tonight?"

He lowered his eyes from hers and looked straight at the wall. "I told them I'd ask you."

She laughed softly and rumpled his hair again. "I'm sorry, darling. But you know what Mrs. Kelsey said about your singing lessons."

Kim pursed his lips. He wished she would not talk about his singing. He didn't want the boys — especially Ron — to hear. But they were just outside the opened door. They must have heard.

"Okay," he said, before she could say any more. "I'll tell them."

He went to the door. "I can't go to-night," he said.

Ron laughed. "Got to practice singing, huh? What're you trying to be — a TV star?"

"Pipe down," Jimmie said. He waved to Kim. "Okay, Kim. We'll see you to-morrow."

" 'Night," said Kim.

He closed the door. When he turned, his mother was still standing there. He saw her eyes blink quickly a few times.

He was a little angry. He wouldn't have cared if Jimmie had come alone. Jimmie was broad-minded. He never kidded Kim about his singing. But Ron had been with him. You couldn't say

26

anything about Kim's singing in front of Ron. Ron took it as a big joke. He razzed Kim every chance he could.

Kim wanted to ask his mother not to speak about his singing in front of Ron again. But from the expression on her face and in her eyes he knew he could not ask her. She was feeling bad already. She must have heard Ron's sarcastic remark.

Kim went to her and put his arms around her waist. A big smile came to his lips.

"Don't feel bad, Mom," he said.

She laid her cheek against his head. "Feel bad? Who says I feel bad?"

He raised his head then. Her eyes looked a little blurry.

She squeezed him tightly, then let him go.

"Okay," she said. "We'd better start. It's Saturday night, and your Aunt Carol and Uncle Jim may come with Barbara Mae."

5

KIM'S mother sat at the black upright piano and played the introduction of a hymn. Kim stood beside her. He really did not feel like singing. He would rather be at the gym practicing basketball. In order to play as well as his teammates, he had to practice as often as they did too. But his singing lessons interfered. Sometimes he wished he had never started singing.

His mother paused at the end of the introduction. He took a deep breath, and started to sing.

Kim sang easily, without strain or effort. It was one of the nice things Mrs. Kelsey said about him. "Kim has the most beautiful soprano voice I have ever heard in my choir," she had told his mother and father one day. "I don't know what I would do without him."

There was a round mirror on the wall to the right of the piano, and in it Kim could see his father's reflection. Mr. O'Connor had laid the newspaper he was reading on his lap, and was listening to Kim while he puffed on his pipe. He caught Kim's eye in the mirror and winked.

"We'll do another one," Kim's mother suggested, "then we'll practice that new piece Mrs. Kelsey wants you to learn."

"Okay," he said.

He sang another song, then practiced the new one. His mother played it through a couple of times. He didn't like the song very much. It was slow. After a while he tired of it.

"Let's quit, Mom," he said.

She looked at him, and smiled. Her eyes flashed like a rainbow with extra blue in it. "All right. It's time to stop, anyway."

"See where the Lions won last night, Kim?" his father asked, as he picked up the paper again.

"Sure," replied Kim. "They beat the Knicks, ninety-seven to ninety-four. That must put them within two games of second place!"

"Right," said his father. "Since you've read all about it, I suppose you know how many points Wally Goodrich scored?"

"Sure! Twenty-eight! He's good, you know it, Dad? I think he's the best in the league!"

His father grinned through the smoke that curled up from his pipe.

6

KIM lay on his stomach on the living-room rug, the sports page of the Sunday newspaper spread before him. It was early and his mother and father were still in bed. Kim was in his pajamas.

The first thing he looked for was the story about yesterday afternoon's Small Fry Basketball game. He wanted to see if his name was mentioned.

At last he found what he was looking for. WINGS, COMETS, WIN IN SMALL FRY, the headline read. A short paragraph told about some of the leading point makers. He saw that Jimmie Burdette had led with twelve points in their game against the Comets.

Underneath were the line-ups of all the teams which had played in the Small Fry League. Their game was third down the list.

	fg	ft	tp
Tikula f	5	0	10
Burdette f	5	2	12
Vargo c	4	3	11
Leonard g	0	1	1
McBride g	1	2	4
O'Connor g	4	1	9
Jordan f	0	0	0
	19	9	47

Kim got a pair of scissors and clipped out the column. Then he took it to his room and placed it in his scrapbook. Flopping in front of the paper again, he began to read about the Seacord Lions. Boy, that Wally Goodrich — thirty-nine points!

Kim's mother came into the living room. She had on a blue quilted house coat. Her hair was in curlers.

"Well!" she greeted him. "Good morning, young man!"

"Good morning, Mom." He smiled.

"I suppose you've got the paper all read?"

"Just the sports page." He rose to his feet. "Think I'll get dressed now."

He started to run to his bedroom and almost bumped into his father, who caught him by the shoulders and laughed.

"Hey! Take it easy!"

Kim smiled. "Good morning, Dad."

"Good morning!" replied Mr. O'Connor. "But it wouldn't have been so good if we had bumped!"

After breakfast they all went to church. Kim climbed the rounding staircase to the choir. Mrs. Kelsey was already there. She was a tall, thin woman with glasses and a very pleasant smile.

"Good morning, Kim," she greeted him.

"Good morning, Mrs. Kelsey," he said, and sat in his regular seat near the front.

In a little while the whole choir was present. Mrs. Kelsey struck the first note on the organ. The low, deep sound boomed throughout the church. Then the choir began to sing. Boys' and girls' voices filled the church.

Little by little the familiar feeling built up inside Kim. He felt the same every time he sang with the choir. His voice seemed to be reaching out to every wall in the big building, to every person sitting in the pews. When he glanced at the boy beside him, the boy smiled, and Kim smiled back. Some of the people who sat below turned and looked up. They saw him, and smiled as they turned away.

He loved to sing with the choir. It was

fun. People enjoyed his singing too, almost as much as he did.

When church was over, he was met by friends outside — grown-up friends, who knew him through his mother and father.

"Your voice is beautiful, Kim," Mrs. Taylor said.

"I wish I had a boy with a voice like yours." Mrs. Osborn smiled. "I'd be real proud of him."

"Thank you," Kim said.

He caught up with his mother and father, and walked home with them.

7

THAT afternoon Jimmie Burdette phoned.

"How about coming to Ron Tikula's place and playing basketball?"

"Tikula's?" Kim made a face.

"He's got a backboard," Jimmie said. "Come on, Kim. He'll let you play."

Kim thought about it a minute. "Well — okay," he answered finally. "I'll see you there."

He told his mother where he was going and changed into his old clothes. Then he ran all the way to Ron Tikula's house. Five boys were there already.

"Kim, Jack, and I will stand you guys," Jimmie Burdette said.

"We'll smear you!" laughed Ron.

As captains, Jimmie and Ron shot fouls to see who would take the ball out first. Jimmie won. He tossed to Jack. Kim broke away from his guard and rushed toward the basket. Jack flung him a hard pass. He caught it and tried a lay-up shot. No good.

"You've got to be better than that, singer!" Ron shouted. He caught the ball and dribbled away from the basket.

Kim pretended he didn't hear.

Ron tried a long shot. It hit the rim and bounded off. Jimmie caught it at the side and banked it in.

A few seconds later Ron's team made a basket. Both teams scored half a dozen times.

Kim was beginning to sweat. It was a cool, wintry day, but he was shifting and running hard.

Kim sank two more buckets.

"Hooray for the singer!" yelled Ron.

Kim's face reddened. He didn't like being kidded all the time about his singing.

"Maybe we ought to tell him this ain't a game for sissies!" Jerry Jordan said when Kim missed some shots.

"Or singers!" said Ron.

Kim stopped running. This was too much. He couldn't keep playing with Ron and Jerry making fun of him. But

he didn't want to run away, either. He glared at Ron.

Jerry was dribbling the ball, and Jimmie was guarding him. Suddenly Ron broke for the basket. Jerry bounced the ball to him. But the ball never got to Ron.

Kim tore in like a shot and caught it. He dribbled once, leaped, and banked the ball off the backboard.

Down it went — through the net!

"Thataboy, Kim!" shouted Jimmie.

Kim looked at Ron. A smile curled his lips.

Ron didn't do any name calling after that.

8

THE Arrows played the Bucs on Wednesday, at 6:30. Kim took Dutchie McBride's place in the second quarter. Dutchie's man had scored six field goals and three free throws. Coach Stickles told Kim to get in there and stop that kid from shooting any more.

Kim tried his best. He found out soon that the boy was one of the fastest he had ever guarded.

At first the boy got away from him twice. But Kim was fast too. He caught up with his man quickly and prevented him from making any baskets.

The half ended with the Bucs ahead, 18 to 10.

In the third quarter Jimmie Burdette showed some of his stuff. He made three drives in that boosted the Arrows' score to 16. Ron sank a long one that tied it up. Then the Bucs rolled for a while and shot their score up to 25.

In the fourth quarter Allan Vargo caught a long pass from Ron and laid it up for a perfect shot. Dutchie came back in and replaced Kim. He was full of pep. He scored four points in less than two minutes and the crowd went wild.

The Bucs scored again, but the Arrows kept going strong. When the final whistle shrilled, the Arrows were ahead, 34 to 32.

On Saturday they beat the Crackerjacks, 52 to 31. But the Crackerjacks were the cellar team, and beating them wasn't anything to brag about.

Kim still missed most of the practices. Coach Stickles asked him once why he didn't come to all of them.

"I have to stay home and practice singing," Kim told him. "And twice a week our choir meets in the church for practice."

It seemed to Kim that Coach Stickles couldn't understand why a boy who liked to play basketball would also like to sing.

"Okay," the coach said. "But it's too

47

bad. You've got the makings of a good basketball player."

Kim knew he would never forget what the coach had said.

In the game against the Rockets, Kim went in when the Rockets were ahead, 8 to 4. It was the first quarter. Kim thought the coach wanted him to stop that tall, dark-haired Rocket from running the score up any higher. He had scored six of the eight points. He looked very good.

The Arrows had the ball. Allan passed it to Ron, who ran down the right side line, stopped, and faked a shot for the basket. A Rocket player jumped in front of him and Rod threw to Kim. Kim pivoted as his man tried to hit the ball from his hands. He kept his back to the boy, and no matter how the Rocket player tried he could not get near the ball.

Kim saw Jimmie break for the basket. Kim leaped off the floor and flung a one-hand pass to him. Jimmie caught it, bounced the ball once, then jumped. A perfect layup!

Jimmie smiled as he and Kim ran up-court. They winked at each other.

Kim ran to cover his man, who was taller than Kim. He seemed to be all legs and arms, but he moved fast. Kim had a tough time keeping between him and the ball.

All at once a long pass sailed up-court toward the Rockets' basket. Kim whirled, and caught his breath. His man had gotten away from him! The tall Rocket player was running to catch the ball, his long white legs pumping up speed.

Kim rushed after him, but the ball sank into the Rocket's hands just before Kim got there. The player spun, started to lift the ball above his head to shoot, then stumbled. He fell against Kim, who reached out his hands to stop him from falling.

The whistle shrilled, Kim whirled. Up the court came the referee holding up two fingers!

Kim stared. "What did I do?"

"Tripping!" said the referee.

"Tripping?" Kim's mouth fell open.

"But I didn't —" He paused. He wouldn't argue with the referee.

"Hey! What's the big idea?" one of the spectators shouted. "The kid tripped himself!"

"Get the ref out of there!" another yelled. "He's blind!"

Kim stepped into his spot behind the white line and waited for the Rocket player to try his two free throws.

The first sank without touching the rim. The second hit the backboard first, then bounded through.

It wasn't my fault, Kim told himself. I hope Coach Stickles knows that.

9

THE coach took Kim and Jimmie out in the second quarter. He didn't say anything to Kim about the personal foul the referee had called on him. It bothered Kim. Maybe the coach thought he had tripped that boy.

Anyway, those two points were the only ones the Rocket player had scored on Kim. But the Rockets were still ahead, 12 to 8. The Arrows could not seem to get going.

A personal foul was called on Ron when he tried to stop a player from making a drive-in shot. The Rocket player made the first free throw. He missed the second. Ron caught the ball and dribbled down-court to the halfway line. He passed to Jordan, who tried a set shot. The ball banked off the board. Bobbie Leonard caught it. He shot, but missed. A Rocket player got the ball and heaved it upcourt.

Kim saw the coach shake his head and strike his fist against his knee. "We're just not lucky today!" he said.

The half ended. ROCKETS — 17, ARROWS — 8.

During the ten-minute intermission Coach Stickles told his boys to stay close to their men when they were on the defensive; not to get rough; to get long shots only when they had to. Pass, pass, pass. Work the ball close to the basket, then shoot.

"Never argue with the referee," he added, "even when he is wrong, as he was when he called that personal on Kim. Sometimes he doesn't see the play from a proper angle, but he has to call it as he sees it."

The words stuck with Kim. No matter if they did lose some of their games, Coach Stickles was a good, smart coach.

Jimmie Burdette started in the second half. He made two baskets, both long shots, but the tall Rocket player with the long arms and legs was dumping them in like marbles into a tomato can.

"It looks as if nobody can stop him

but you, Kim!" the coach said. "Get in there!"

Kim got in there. He didn't stop the tall boy altogether from making baskets. The boy sank two for four points. But that was all. And Kim had scored three points. All in all, it wasn't bad for eight minutes of play — two in the third quarter, six in the last.

The Arrows finished on the short end, 36 to 28.

10

THE line-up was in the paper the next day. Kim clipped it out as another treasure for his scrapbook.

One sentence was in fine print about a Rocket player who had scored the most points. Another sentence told about Allan and Jimmie both scoring eight points for the Arrows. Kim read every word, hoping there might be something written about him. But there wasn't.

He looked at the clipping again.

	fg	ft	tp
Tikula f	2	3	7
Burdette f	3	2	8
Vargo c	3	2	8
Leonard g	1	0	2
O'Connor g	1	1	3
Jordan f	0	0	0
	10	8	28

Well, at least he was playing as much as the others, even though he didn't practice as often.

If he could only practice more he'd make more baskets. Maybe Coach Stickles would put him in as forward.

But he — he had to attend choir practice, and practice singing at home. That was what took his time. Suppose he did not sing. He could attend all the basketball practices then. He could develop a good eye for shots. You don't have to be tall to be a good shot. Jimmie Burdette wasn't tall, was he?

Kim's mother came into the room. She had on a dark blue dress with a black patent-leather belt around the waist, and the new blue shoes Daddy had bought her for Christmas.

Kim thought of how much she loved to hear him sing. He remembered how she looked when she sat at the piano playing for him. She looked as happy as on her birthday when Daddy gave her a gift. Kim knew that no matter what happened, he would never give up singing.

His mother asked, "Don't you think you'd better get dressed?"

His eyes widened. "Where are we going?"

She smiled. "It's a surprise," she said. "Get dressed. We'll tell you later."

He didn't like to be teased. It made him excited.

"Oh, Mom!" he cried. "Please tell me!"

Then his dad came in. He had on a white shirt and a flashy yellow necktie. He was holding three tickets in his hand.

Kim's heart jumped. Now he knew!

"We're going to the Lions-Philadelphia game!" he cried.

"Right!" laughed his father.

11

KIM watched the big gymnasium fill up with people. Music blared from loud-speakers. Boys sold programs. Kim's dad bought one for him.

"I'll keep score!" Kim said breathlessly. "Got a pencil, Dad?"

His father gave him a pencil.

The Philadelphia Ravens trotted out onto the floor. They were dressed in yellow jackets and long yellow pants. They had four basketballs which they began to throw at the basket. Kim watched excitedly. There must be a dozen men on that team!

After a while the Seacord Lions trotted in. They were in bright green. Everybody cheered and whistled.

"There's Thompson!" cried Kim. He knew most of the players from watching them on television. "And there's Wally Goodrich! See him, Dad? See him? Boy! Just watch him!"

The players on both teams began to remove their jackets. That made them look even taller than before. Thompson must be about six feet six. Reynolds, six feet seven. Kim was sure Wally Goodrich was six feet four. He knew more about Wally than he did about any of the others.

Kim opened the program and found the players' names. Wally Goodrich, 24 years old, six feet four inches. He was right. He read through the others. Wow! Such giants! Philadelphia had a man six feet nine! A player like that had only to hold the ball over the basket and drop it in!

Two referees appeared. They wore black pants and black and white striped shirts. The music stopped playing. An announcer spoke. He gave the names of the starting players of both teams. Then the national anthem was played and everybody stood up. When it was over, the people sat down.

The game began.

All the players wore jerseys and shorts

now. A referee tossed the ball up between the two giant centers. Long fingers tapped it. Philadelphia got it,
passed it to another Philadelphian. A
Lion player snared it!

Kim jumped to his feet. "Wally
Goodrich caught it, Daddy! That was
Wally —"

His heart thumped like a hammer
against his ribs. He sat on the edge of
his chair, one hand gripping the program, the other the chair in front of
him. Wally dribbled the ball down-
court, running as if he were carrying
the ball. All at once he passed. The
next second the ball was passed back
to him. He leaped for a hook shot.
Made it!

"See, Dad?" cried Kim. "He's good!"

The ball was passed upcourt. Kim had trouble keeping track of it. These players moved with the speed of lightning. A basket was made almost every five seconds. First the Ravens made one or two. Then the Lions did. It was too fast for Kim to put down on paper. He stuck the pencil into his pocket. He could not watch the game and keep score too.

When the half ended, the score was SEACORD LIONS — 48, PHILADELPHIA RAVENS — 47.

During the intermission a Philadelphia player was named the outstanding player of the month, and given a wrist watch.

"Wally Goodrich was outstanding player last month," Kim said.

The second half was as lively and exciting as the first. Substitutes came in often. Wally Goodrich went out and then came back in two or three times. Kim enjoyed the way he faked when a guard came up to him. Twice he bounced the ball behind him with his right hand and continued bouncing it, without interruption, with his left. Another time he faked an overhand pass. When the guard jumped, Wally dribbled under his arm and laid one up for an easy two points. It looked easy, anyway.

Kim noticed that Wally shot his fouls with one hand. He would raise the ball to his right shoulder with both hands, then push the ball up with his right hand. He made it almost every time.

Just before the game was over, Kim asked his father for a favor. His father smiled and nodded.

The score was still close when the game ended. The Seacord Lions won, 101 to 98.

When they went home, Kim had a name scribbled in pencil on the back of his program.

It was *Wally Goodrich*.

12

O N the following nights, as he practiced singing at home and with the choir, Kim thought about the team practicing basketball in the gym. Some of those players, like Allan and Jimmie, might one day play for the Lions. They practiced all the time. Sometimes he could not understand how they got such good marks in school. But they studied too, of course.

Then, on Friday, his mother let him skip his singing lesson to practice basketball. He hurried eagerly to the gym.

"Look who's here!" Ron Tikula yelled. "The singing boy from Tim-buck-toy!"

"The future TV star!" Jerry Jordan cried, and began to mock him. "Car-ry me ba-a-ck . . ."

"All right, boys! Cut it out!" Coach Stickles yelled.

Kim thought about that in church Sunday, just before he began to sing. He thought about it so much an ache grew into a big ball in his throat. He brushed a tear from his eye and hoped that nobody had seen it.

He didn't think he'd be able to sing after that. But after Mrs. Kelsey played the introduction, he lifted his voice in song. It flowed from his lips as easily as a bird taking off in flight. The longer he sang the less he thought about Ron Tikula, Jerry Jordan, and everything connected with basketball.

The heavy weight in his heart melted away. The hurt in his throat disappeared.

13

KIM missed basketball practice Monday night because he had to rehearse with the choir.

After rehearsal Mrs. Kelsey said, "Starting on Thursday, two weeks before Easter Sunday, we will learn some new hymns. I hope none of you will miss any of those rehearsals. Easter is an extra-special day. We'll want our choir to sing extra-special too. Right?"

"Right!" everyone answered almost together.

The following morning thick flakes of

snow dropped lazily from the sky. It was about six inches deep on the sidewalk, and soft as swan's-down.

Kim met Jane Armbruster on the street corner and they walked to school together. Jane was in his grade.

"What beautiful snow!" she cried happily. "I think I'll go skiing tonight at the park!"

Her cheeks were almost as red as her snowsuit.

"If I had skis I'd go too," Kim said.

She turned big dark eyes to him. A snowflake fell on her nose. "You can use mine! We can take turns!"

He shook his head. "No, thanks. I can't ski, anyway."

"You can learn!"

He didn't know how to tell her that he didn't want to go because she was a girl. Of course, if Jimmie Burdette or some of the other boys went he would go. Anyway, he decided, he wouldn't want to borrow her skis. He would certainly be teased then!

Bang! A snowball hit him on the shoulder!

He heard a laugh behind him. Another snowball brushed his sleeve and buried itself in the snow on the sidewalk.

"All right, Ron!" he yelled.

It was Ron Tikula and Dutchie McBride, grinning like Cheshire cats. They were making more snowballs.

"Let's run!" Jane said.

"Run, nothing!" cried Kim. "I'll give

it right back to them! Here — take my books!"

She took his books. He bent over and scooped up a handful of snow, quickly formed it into a hard-packed ball, and threw it at Ron. Ron tried to dodge, but he couldn't move fast enough in the deep snow and the snowball hit him.

"Good shot!" Jane said.

The boys threw snowballs back and forth for a minute. Then Ron shouted, "Okay! We've had enough!"

He and Dutchie cheerfully came up to Jane and Kim. Ron wore a leather jacket and a hat with ear flaps. Dutchie had on a navy-blue pea jacket. His hat was somewhat like Ron's.

"Going to the clinic, Kim?" Ron asked.

He was nice, now. Maybe it was because Jane was with them.

"What clinic?" said Kim.

"The basketball clinic. The Lions are putting it on tomorrow night. Oh, that's right. You weren't at our practice last night. Coach Stickles told us about it."

Kim's forehead creased. "What's a basketball clinic?"

"Don't you know?" Dutchie said. "It's where they teach you how to play basketball."

"Maybe Kim thinks he knows enough about it already." Ron was poking fun at him.

Kim glared at Ron. He took the books from Jane.

"Thanks, Jane," he said quietly.

Then he looked at Ron and Dutchie. "Are you guys going?"

"The coach said that everybody should go," Ron said. "My father's taking me."

"I'm going with Ron," Dutchie said.

"Well — I'd like to go too," admitted Kim. "I sure would!"

14

KIM didn't have to persuade his father to take him to the clinic. Mr. O'Connor had read about it in the paper, and agreed at once that it might be good for Kim. Jimmie Burdette went with them.

The clinic was held in the school where most of the Small Fry Basketball games were played. About a thousand boys from seven to high school age attended it. Most of the smaller boys were with their parents. All the Lion players were there, dressed in their regular uniforms.

Kim sat in the middle row of seats halfway up one side. He thought he would like to be on the court with the ten or twelve boys who were receiving personal instruction from the Lion players. But soon he found that he could learn as much just sitting and watching. Maybe more. For he could look from one small group to another.

The way it was done was simple. Two or three Lion players worked with two or three boys who volunteered from the crowd. The boys were mostly Small Fry Basketball size. Kim recognized some of them.

Wally Goodrich, Dick Wynn, and Stretch Thompson were showing a group how to make layup shots. It was easy for the Lions, since the baskets were lower than the height at which they played.

First the Lions would show how to make the shots, then the boys would try to do the same. At the other basket three other Lion players were showing boys the drive-in play. Kim enjoyed that. It was a hard one. You had to rush in under the basket, raise your shoulders way up, then your arms, and shoot. In a game a player might easily foul you. If you made the basket you would be allowed one free throw. If you missed the basket, two free throws.

Many other plays were shown: set shots; hook shots; free throws; how to keep the ball close to the floor when you dribble; the different ways of passing a ball; how to guard your man; how not to "walk" with the ball.

The Lions seemed to be explaining and showing everything about how to play basketball. Kim was sorry the clinic had to end.

"Boy! That was wonderful!" he said to his father as they walked out of the gym with the crowd of boys and parents.

His father grinned. "Did you like it, Jimmie?"

"Did I? I learned something about dribbling. I always bounced the ball too high. I'm going to practice to keep it down."

"Thataboy!" said Mr. O'Connor.

15

KIM did not forget what he had learned at the clinic. Coach Stickles had taught him a lot too, but he had missed too many practices.

What he had seen at the basketball clinic stayed in his mind better than the things Coach Stickles had told him. When he told his dad this, Mr. O'Connor smiled and said:

"Maybe it's because the Seacord Lions were the teachers!"

"Maybe!" laughed Kim.

The Arrows were not doing too well.

They had been in third place for a while. Now they were back in fourth.

Kim felt he wasn't doing very well either. Oh, he had a lot of hustle, of course. Coach Stickles had said so, and Kim remembered that all right.

"Well, next Saturday afternoon is our last game," said Coach Stickles after they had won their second game with the Comets. "If we win, we'll be in second place and eligible for the play-offs. If we lose, we'll be in third or fourth. Depends on how the other teams make out."

"What happens if we get in the play-offs?" Dutchie asked. He hadn't played with the Arrows last year. He didn't know.

Coach Stickles smiled. "We'll play the team which comes in first place two out of three games."

"What does the winner get?" Ron Tikula asked. "A trophy — like last year?"

"That's right. A trophy," the coach said. "We'll put it in the showcase in our clubroom. Also, each boy gets a basketball pin. So if you fellas want that trophy and those pins real bad, you've got to play the best basketball you can! How about it?"

"We sure will!" they yelled all together.

The Arrows' last game was against the Rockets. Coach Stickles started Kim at guard position. The coach kept him in four minutes of the first quarter, then had Bobbie Leonard play the remaining two minutes. Scoring was quite even. It was 18 to 17, in the Rockets' favor, when the quarter ended.

Kim went back in the second quarter. He watched his man like a hawk. When Kim got the ball, he dribbled close to the floor. He ran down-court like a fawn chased by a fox. He stopped, faked a throw that put his man off guard, then shot at the basket from his favorite position.

A bucket!

"Thataboy, singer!" Ron Tikula shouted.

Kim pretended he didn't hear.

All the way through the game the

lead shifted first to the Arrows, then to the Rockets. Coach Stickles was giving everybody on the team a chance to play. Some played only a minute. Everybody on the first team was out one time or another.

There were ten seconds left to play when Allan Vargo shot a pass to Kim. Kim dribbled down-court, then passed to Ron. The score was 53 to 52, in the Rockets' favor. This was the Arrows' last chance to win.

Kim dashed toward the basket. Ron threw the ball to him. Kim caught it, and leaped for a jump shot. Just then a Rocket player hit his arm. The slap could be heard nearly all through the court.

The whistle shrilled. The referee held up two fingers, which meant that Kim was allowed two shots.

Kim stepped to the free-throw line. The referee waited till both sides were ready, then gave the ball to Kim and moved out of the way.

Kim held the ball in both his hands, looked at the basket. It seemed so high, so small. He took a deep breath, turned the ball around in his hands till it felt just right, then threw.

The ball hit the backboard, rolled around the rim, and fell off!

The crowd groaned.

"Come on, Kim!" cried Ron. "Make it this time!"

The referee got the ball, waited till

the teams were ready again, then handed it to Kim.

Kim took another deep breath. He could feel the sweat rolling down his neck. What a moment! Why did it have to be him trying these foul shots? Why couldn't it have been Jimmie, who was really good at making them?

Kim brushed the hair back from his forehead. He turned the ball a little in his hands, then bent his knees slightly, straightened them, and shot the ball toward the basket.

It sailed in a slow, beautiful arch. Right through the basket without touching the rim!

This time the crowd screamed.

The score was tied, 53 to 53!

Then the whistle shrilled. The two referees talked things over. Then one of them called the captains of both teams together and said that an overtime period of two minutes would be played.

The Rockets took out the ball. They passed upcourt, fumbled. Jimmie Burdette retrieved it. He dribbled a few steps, passed to Kim. Kim passed to Ron. A Rocket player intercepted, dribbled upcourt, stopped, and passed.

Kim jumped, hit the ball with his hand, bounced it, and shot a long pass to Jimmie, who was running for the Arrows' basket.

Jimmie caught the ball, raced for the basket, and jumped high for a layup shot.

A bucket!

A few seconds later the game ended. The Arrows won — 55 to 53.

Jimmie pounded Kim on the back. "We're in the play-offs, Kim!"

Kim smiled broadly.

16

SUNDAY afternoon Kim received an invitation to Barbara Mae Pletz's birthday party. Barbara Mae was his cousin. Her mother and father, Aunt Carol and Uncle Jim, were favorites of his. They never forgot *his* birthday, either. The party was to be next Saturday afternoon. Aunt Carol would want him to sing.

Kim didn't like that very much. But he supposed he would sing anyway. Funny how some people made such a fuss about a kid singing.

Later that evening Coach Stickles came to the house. He wore a felt hat and a topcoat. His cheeks were red from the cold. But he had a happy smile.

"Well, how does it feel to be in the play-offs?" he asked Kim.

"Good, Coach!" Kim grinned.

Kim's father invited the coach into the living room. The coach did not take off his coat because he couldn't stay long, he said. But he stayed an hour. They just talked about basketball.

"When do we play?" Kim asked.

"I don't know yet," the coach said. "We're having a meeting tomorrow night to decide. I'll let you know."

On Tuesday evening the coach telephoned. "Kim, be at the gym at one o'clock, Saturday. We're playing the Seals. The game starts at two, but we want everybody there early. Okay?"

"Okay!" said Kim.

Kim shook with excitement. He called up Jimmie Burdette and they talked for five minutes. Jimmie was as excited as he was.

When Kim hung up, his mother was standing beside him. She had a worried look on her face. Kim stared at her.

"What's the matter, Mom?" he said.

She answered quietly. "Barbara Mae's birthday party is Saturday afternoon."

Kim's heart went to pieces. He had forgotten about the party! He whirled before his mother could see the tears fill his eyes.

And then he had an idea.

He dried the tears and turned to his mother. "Mom, do you suppose Aunt Carol would change the time of the party to Saturday morning if I asked her?"

His mother looked at him thoughtfully. "Well, it certainly won't hurt to ask her!" She smiled. "Go ahead. Call her now."

Kim went to the phone. Suddenly he was very scared. Suppose Aunt Carol had a very good reason not to change the time. What then?

He looked at his mother. She smiled encouragingly.

"Go on," she said. "Pick up the receiver."

Kim picked it up. He dialed Aunt Carol's number. He heard the phone ringing.

Soon a voice answered. "Hello?"

"Aunt Carol?"

"Oh, it's you, Kim!" she cried. "How are you?"

"I'm fine," Kim said. "Aunt Carol, our — our basketball team has to play Saturday afternoon. Can't you change the party to Saturday morning?"

"Well — I don't know." Aunt Carol seemed surprised. "Why, is it an important game, Kim?"

"It sure is, Aunt Carol. It's our first game in the play-offs. And if we don't win, we're out."

"Say! Never let it be said that your

Aunt Carol caused the Arrows to lose their first play-off game! Hang up, and I'll start calling all the mothers right away!"

An hour later she called back. "Kim?"

"Yes, Aunt Carol?" he said excitedly.

"I got them all but Mrs. Wood," she said. "I can call her tomorrow. They all say they can have their children here Saturday morning. How do you feel now?"

"Much better, Aunt Carol! Thanks! Boy, you're sure swell, Aunt Carol!"

There was a smile in Aunt Carol's voice.

"The point is, Kim," she said, "your Uncle Jim and I would like to see that game too!"

17

THE birthday party was a real success. Barbara Mae received many beautiful gifts. The girls and boys had a good time playing Pin the Donkey's Tail, Guess Who, and many other games. Everybody won prizes. And Kim sang.

He sang a few solos. The children joined in when he sang songs which they knew.

Then it was time to go to the gym. The Seals wore yellow jerseys, the Arrows blue. Kim was in the starting line-up. The Seals caught the tap from center and passed the ball back and forth upcourt toward their basket. Kim guarded his man every second. He seemed tied to him.

A Seal player shot for the basket, and missed. Kim leaped high and caught the rebound. He tossed to Jimmie Burdette, who passed to Ron. The ball moved fast down-court. A pass was thrown to Jimmie under the basket. Jimmie leaped for a layup.

Two points!

The Arrows sank two more before the Seals got going. In the second quarter Kim was taken out, and Dutchie McBride went in. Dutchie scored three points, a layup and a foul shot. The Arrows led at the half, 28 to 19.

The second half started with Kim back in guard position. His man now was a redhead with freckles. The redhead kept bumping Kim with his hip. Kim gave him a dirty look but said nothing.

Ron sank in a set shot. Then the Seals went crazy and piled up eight points. Ron committed a foul and the Seal player rang up another point.

Score: ARROWS — 30, SEALS — 27.

Kim was getting angry. His man was still bumping him with his hip. Once he struck Kim with his elbow. Kim thought the redhead did it on purpose, but he wasn't sure.

"I have to make the referee see him bumping me," thought Kim. "But how?"

The Seals were passing the ball up-court. In the backcourt the ball went wild, zoomed out of bounds. Kim took it out, bounced to Ron Tikula. The Arrows whipped the ball back and forth till it was near their basket.

Then Jimmie whipped the ball to Kim. Kim feinted toward the basket, then broke around the redheaded Seal player. As he went by, the redhead bumped him with his hip.

The whistle pierced the hall. Foul!

Kim stepped slowly to the free-throw line. He looked briefly at the redheaded player, saw a scowl on the boy's freckled face. Kim smiled to himself. The referee gave him the ball.

Kim took his time, and made the shot.

Both teams scored six more points before the third quarter ended.

Score: ARROWS — 37, SEALS — 33.

Kim didn't start the fourth quarter. When there were three minutes left of the game, he replaced Dutchie.

The Seals were playing hard. But the Arrows kept up their pace. A foul on Kim helped the Seals gain another point.

And then all at once the whistle blew.

The first game of the play-offs was over, the Arrows winning, 46 to 43.

Now all they had to do was win one out of the next two games.

Kim knew it wouldn't be easy.

18

COACH Stickles told the boys that the second game of the play-offs was scheduled for next Thursday night. If the Arrows won, it was all over. The Arrows would be champs. If they lost, the last game would be played Saturday afternoon.

"Boy, I hope we win," Dutchie said excitedly.

"Don't worry," said Ron. "We will!"

Then, on Monday evening, Mrs. Kelsey telephoned Kim.

"I just want to remind you of choir practice Thursday night, Kim," she said.

"A week from next Sunday is Easter, remember."

Kim stared. "Already?" His heart sank.

The second play-off game was on Thursday night. Couldn't Mrs. Kelsey have practice some other night besides Thursday?

But Mrs. Kelsey was not a person to change a date once she had made plans for it.

Kim knew how much the choir meant to Mrs. Kelsey. He knew Mrs. Kelsey would want him very much to be there. But that wasn't all. His mother would want him to be there too.

"Are you still there, Kim?" Mrs. Kelsey asked.

Kim laughed. "Yes, I am, Mrs. Kelsey. Okay. I'll be at the church Thursday night. Good night, Mrs. Kelsey."

"Thank you. And good night, Kim."

"Who was that?" asked Mrs. O'Connor after Kim had hung up.

"Mrs. Kelsey," said Kim. "We're having choir practice Thursday night."

Mrs. O'Connor's brows arched. "Isn't that the night the Arrows are playing their second play-off game?"

"Yes, Mom," said Kim.

"What are you going to do?"

"I'm going to practice."

His mother's face brightened. Her eyes filled with warmth. She ruffled Kim's hair and smiled.

On Wednesday, after school, Kim

went to Coach Stickles's house. He was scared. He felt sure the coach would not like it when he heard that Kim would not be able to play in Thursday night's game.

Mrs. Stickles opened the door. She was a small dark-haired woman with sparkling blue eyes.

"Hello, Kim!" she said.

"Is Coach Stickles in?" Kim asked nervously.

"Yes, he is. Come in."

Coach Stickles was sitting in the living room. He smiled at Kim, got up, and shook Kim's hand.

"This is a surprise, Kim," he said. "Sit down. What's on your mind?"

Kim sat down. He was so frightened

of what the coach might say that he held one hand tight in the other.

"I can't play basketball Thursday night, Coach," he said finally.

Coach Stickles frowned. "Why not, Kim?"

"I've got choir practice," Kim replied. "It's special for Easter Sunday. I'd a lot like to play in that game, Coach, but I think I should be at that rehearsal. I — I thought I'd tell you."

Kim looked up. He was squeezing his hand tighter than ever now.

The coach said nothing for a long while. He looked at Mrs. Stickles, and then at Kim. Suddenly a broad smile spread across his face.

"Kim," he said, "as much as I should

like to have you play, I'm glad you chose to practice with your choir."

Kim's eyes widened. "You — you mean you're not mad?"

"Mad? Not at all, Kim. I know how much you'd like to play in that second play-off game. It takes a lot of, well — courage — to make the decision you made. Matter of fact, I'm kind of proud of you for it."

Kim's eyes shone. He had never dreamed that the coach would say things like that!

"Thanks, Coach!" he said.

On Thursday night Kim went to choir rehearsal. Mrs. Kelsey and all the boys and girls were happy to see him. They knew he had chosen to sing with them instead of playing basketball.

The moment Kim began to sing he became happy too. The voices around him were like the rays of the sun warming his heart. He enjoyed the rehearsal so much he never minded at all that he had not played basketball that night.

The following day he found out that the Seals had won the game. They had beaten the Arrows 38 to 29.

Kim had only one good feeling about that. The Arrows and the Seals would tangle again Saturday, and he would be in the game.

19

THE last and important game was on Saturday. The Arrows met the Seals again on the same court. And what a crowd! The place was jammed!

"Guess who I saw sitting in the stands?" Ron said to Kim.

"Who?" asked Kim.

"Mrs. Kelsey!"

Kim stared. "Mrs. Kelsey?" He turned to look, but among all the hundreds of faces he couldn't spot hers. "I didn't think she cared for basketball," he said curiously.

The game got off to a fast start. The Seals drew first blood, but the Arrows came right back and scored two baskets one after the other. They were hot. By the end of the first quarter they had run their score up to 13, six ahead of the Seals.

The second quarter was a little different. The Arrows still kept the lead, but the half ended with the scoreboard showing ARROWS — 23, SEALS — 19.

The third quarter started with Jerry Jordan in place of Jimmie Burdette, and Dutchie McBride in place of Kim.

Before the quarter ended, the coach put Kim and Jimmie in. The game was getting closer every second. Both teams were playing tight ball, throwing passes carefully, taking shots only when they were near their basket.

By the middle of the fourth quarter the score was tied, 37 to 37.

Time was called. Coach Stickles walked out onto the court and talked with his boys.

"Don't be nervous," he said. "Just play the best you can. You're doing fine. I'm proud of every one of you."

He paused. "When there are only two minutes left to play, try some long shots. But still use two hands. And remember — win or lose — you boys are still my team. Good luck!"

He turned and walked off the court.

The boys looked at each other.

"There's one great guy," Jimmie said.

"I hate to let him down," said Kim.

"If you practiced more with us, instead of with that choir," broke in Ron Tikula, "maybe we wouldn't have it so tough."

"Cut it out," snapped Jimmie. "This is no time to talk like that."

Ron slapped Kim lightly on the leg. He laughed. "Oh, heck, I'm only kidding."

The time-in whistle blew.

The Seals took out the ball. They passed it upcourt.

Ron leaped in and tried to take the ball away from a Seal guard. He was a little rough. He pushed the guard. The referee blew his whistle.

Foul!

The Seal was allowed one shot. He took his time — made it.

The Seals went ahead, 38 to 37.

The Seals' rooters cheered.

Kim looked at the clock. One and a half minutes to go!

All at once a song rose from the Arrows' rooters' side of the gym — a song from the throats of ten to fifteen boys and girls, led by a woman whose high soprano voice Kim recognized immediately.

> We came to see the Arrows win!
> Arrows win! Arrows win!
> We came to see the Arrows win,
> And carry home the tro-phy!
> Hip-hip! Hooray!
> Hip-hip! Hooray!
> Hip-hip! Hooray!

Kim looked up at the sea of sparkling faces. A flock of white hands rose and waved at him.

Kim's face brightened. Imagine Mrs. Kelsey and the choir doing that for the Arrows! Who would have thought —

Kim turned his attention back to the game.

Jordan took the ball out for the Arrows. He bounced it to Ron. Ron passed to Kim. Kim wanted to pass, but all his teammates were well guarded.

He dribbled down-court. All at once he was trapped. Seals surrounded him.

Then he saw a figure in blue running clear of the others. It was Allan. Kim leaped, snapped the ball. Allan caught it.

In an instant the Seals swarmed around Allan. Kim knew there were only seconds left to go in the game. Breathlessly he raced down the side line.

Allan held the ball high, pivoting on one foot, while he looked for a free man to throw the ball to.

Like a bolt of lightning, Kim swooped in front of his man. Allan whipped the ball to him.

Kim caught it, dribbled toward the basket. But he couldn't shoot. Two Seals got in front of him, jumping around him so fast they seemed to be all arms and legs.

There wasn't much time. Only seconds —

Kim whirled, then leaped off the floor. At the same time he turned his shoulder so that he faced the basket.

He spotted Allan beyond the basket, waving his right arm. Kim shot the ball to him. Allan caught it, leaped for the basket, and with one hand tried a layup.

The ball banked against the backboard, and arched down through the net!

Scarcely had the ball dropped into a Seal player's hands, when the whistle blew, announcing the end of the game!

The Arrows had won the Small Fry Basketball Championship, 39 to 38!

The Arrows' fans screamed lustily. Kim saw Mrs. Kelsey and the choir and the whole Arrows' rooting section standing on their feet and waving their arms with joy. He saw his mother and father too, and Aunt Carol, Uncle Jim, and Barbara Mae. They were standing and cheering their hearts out.

Kim choked. Boy! he thought. Oh, boy!

Coach Stickles shook Kim's hand in the dressing room.

"I won't say that without you the Arrows cannot win a game, Kim," he said, "but this I'm sure of: We would not have won the game tonight without the choir. They sure gave us the help we needed."

Kim could only smile.

After both teams showered and dressed, they were invited for supper at the Markson Hotel. The commissioner of the league gave a speech, and said that next week a banquet would be held in honor of the champion Arrows. At that time the trophy would be given to them, and to each Arrow player an award pin.

"And you runners-up, the Seals, are invited too," the commissioner added, smiling. "You boys played a wonderful game. Until the very last second nobody really knew who was going to win. So, for each one of you, an award pin also."

That made the Seals feel pretty good. They just smiled at each other. But the Arrows, to show their appreciation, clapped and cheered for them.

Ron was sitting on Kim's left. After

the commissioner sat down, Ron leaned toward Kim and said, "You know who should be given a pin too?"

Kim frowned. "Who?"

"That choir you're in. If they hadn't been there, maybe we wouldn't have won!"

For a moment Kim thought Ron was poking fun at him and the choir again.

But the longer he looked at Ron, the more certain he was that Ron meant every word he said. Kim could tell by Ron's eyes, and the serious smile on Ron's lips.

That night, when Kim got off the bus near his house, Ron shouted out, "Good night, Kimmy, pal! See you to-morrow!"

Kim knew then that Ron would not make fun of him any more.

As he headed for the front porch, where a light was burning for him, a tune popped into Kim's mind. And then suddenly he began singing:

> We came to see the Arrows win!
> Arrows win! Arrows win!
> We came to see the Arrows win,
> And carry home the tro-phy!